DAISY the Dancing Cow

Viki Woodworth

Boyds Mills Press

To Nora and Charlotte—my hoofers

—Mom

Text and illustrations copyright © 2003 by Viki Woodworth

Published by Boyds Mills Press, Inc.
A Highlights Company
815 Church Street
Honesdale, Pennsylvania 18431
Printed in China

Publisher Cataloging-in-Publication Data (U.S.)

Woodworth, Viki.
　　Daisy the dancing cow / written and illustrated by Viki Woodworth.— 1st ed.
[32]p. : col. ill. ;　cm.
Summary: When a dancer in a local show takes ill, Daisy, a cow, comes to the rescue.
ISBN 1-59078-059-0
1. Cows—Fiction. 2. Dancers—Fiction. I. Title.
　[E]　AC　2003
2002117185

First edition, 2003
The text of this book is set in 16-point Usherwood Book.

Visit our Web site at www.boydsmillspress.com

10 9 8 7 6 5 4 3 2 1

As Daisy passed the Corn County Theatre, she heard swinging music and loud tapping sounds. "What's that?" she wondered.

She read the sign on the theatre door:

HOOFERS NEEDED FOR MUSICAL SHOW. AUDITIONS TODAY.

"Oooh," thought Daisy. "Am I a hoofer? I have a hoof. I have four."

She peered inside. A woman on stage called out, "Stomp, hop, step, flap," while people waved their arms and tapped their feet.

"That looks like fun!" thought Daisy. "I want to do that."

She tried. Stomp, hop, step, CRASH!

Everyone stopped and stared.
"What is this cow doing here?" demanded the director.

Daisy smiled earnestly. She pointed to the audition sign, then to her hoof.

The director scowled. "Hoofers do not have hooves. Hoofers are dancers. You are a cow, and no cow will dance in my show!"

Daisy's lips quivered. Then one dancer came forward.

"We do need a gofer, Ms. Director."

Daisy's eyes grew wide. "A gofer," she thought. "That sounds glamorous!"

"I suppose a cow can be a gofer," said the director. She tossed Daisy some money. "Go for coffee," she said.

"Welcome aboard," said the dancer. "I'm Nina. I'll show you how to go for coffee."

After they returned with the coffee, Daisy watched the dancers kick and spin. "Being a gofer is exciting," she thought. "But being a hoofer looks magical. I wish I could dance."

In between gofer jobs, Nina showed Daisy around the theatre. Daisy learned how to pull the curtain up and let it back down.

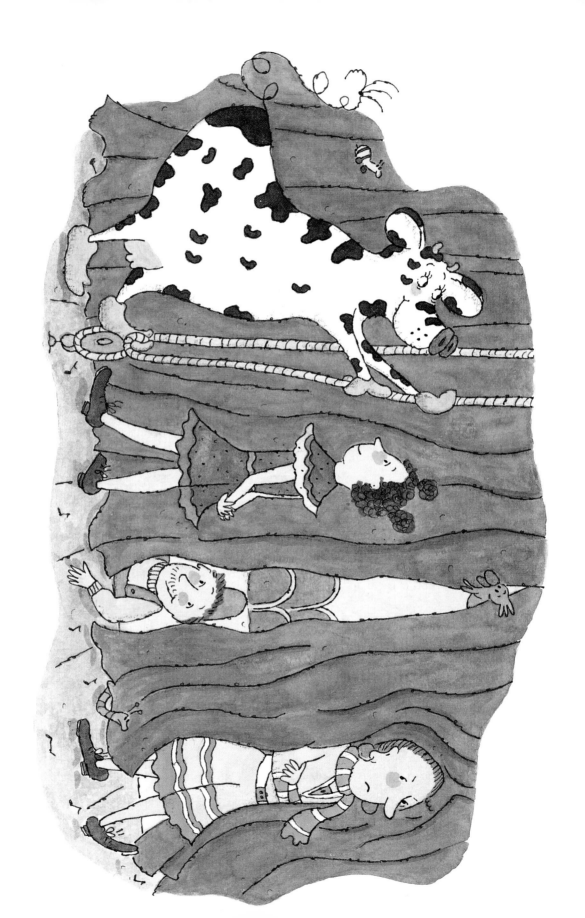

And how to do a shuffle.

She learned how to put on makeup.

And how to do the Shim-Sham.

She learned how to sew costumes.

And how to do the Triple-Time Step.
After a while, Daisy knew all the dances.

The night of the performance finally arrived.
As Nina ran up the backstage steps, she tripped.
"Ooo-ow!" Nina cried. "I hurt my ankle! I can't dance!
The show will be ruined!"

Daisy carried Nina into the theatre.
"What can I do to help?" Daisy thought. "I could dance Nina's part, but the director won't let a cow in her show." Then she had an idea.

She rushed backstage and rummaged. "Perfect," she said. "The director will never know it's me."

Daisy sailed onto the stage just in time.

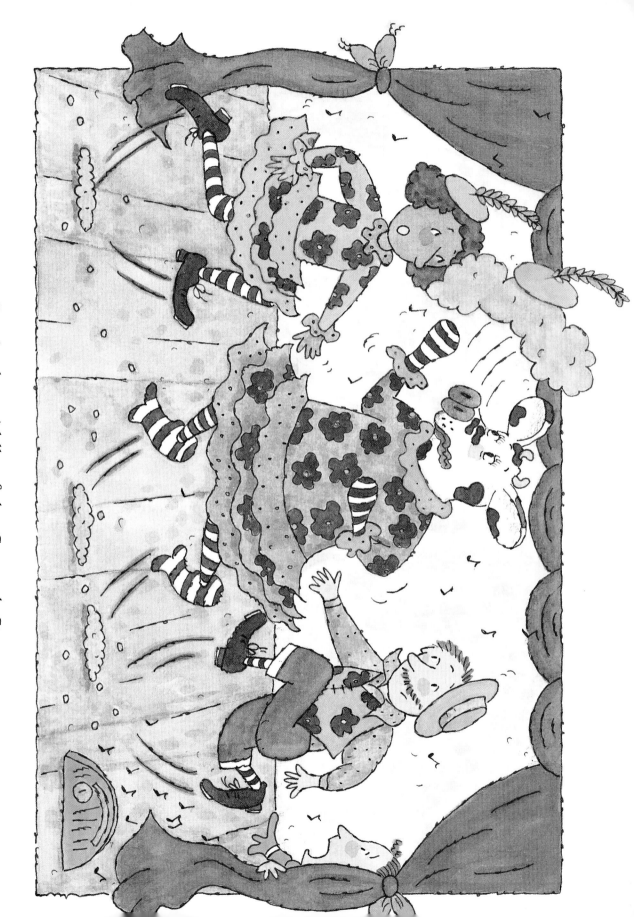

But in the middle of the Corncob Stomp, her wig flew off. The director gasped.

Daisy froze. She looked at the director. She looked at Nina. Then she thought, "The show must go on!"

She stomped.

She hopped.

She danced divinely.

When the curtain came down, the director stormed over.

"Oh, no," thought Daisy. "She's furious!"

"Of all the . . .," sputtered the director. "I never . . . you, you, you . . ."

"You amazing cow! You saved the show!
Will you join our dance troupe?"

Daisy did a twirl and a shuffle and several Shim-Shams. "Moo-ee," she thought. "I'm a hoofer!"